SMOKE TREE SERIES NOVELLA

HORSE HUNTS

GARY J. GEORGE

For Ginny, without whom
there would be no point to this.

A WORD FOR READERS ABOUT THE WAY
THE AUTHOR USES QUOTATION MARKS
IN DIALOGUE

Dialogue in this novel opens with quotation marks, as is usual. However, what follows sometimes differs from convention. If the person speaks for more than one paragraph, he does not put quotation marks before each new paragraph, and he does not close the quotation marks until that person has finished speaking.

NOVEMBER 1960

DAY ONE

In November of 1960, Lieutenant Carlos Caballo, commander of the Smoke Tree substation of the San Bernardino County Sheriff's department, was sitting at his desk, absorbed in thought. Lieutenant Caballo, known to almost everyone in the Lower Colorado River Basin as "Horse," was devising a plan to track down an important piece of evidence in the house of three murders case when his intercom buzzed.

"Yes, Fred."

"Shooting at Vidal Junction. At the agricultural inspection station. One of the inspectors thought a guy coming in from Arizona was acting a little nervous, so he had him pull over and get out of the car. When the inspector told the driver to open his trunk, the man pulled out a gun and shot him, then jumped in and drove off in our direction.

They called the California Highway Patrol, but the officer assigned to that beat was closer to Desert Center than Vidal when he got the call. By the time the patrolman got on 95, he found the car abandoned. Ran out of gas or broke down. Looks like the shooter may be on foot in the desert."

Horse picked up his hat and went into the outer office.

"I'm on my way, but I need you to do some things.

Call Jim Harkness and Andy Chesney and tell them they're about to get some overtime. Have them get their horses and meet me out there."

"Yes, sir. I'm on it."

"And Fred, Chesney has a double trailer. Have him go by my place and get my horse and my tack. Canyon is in the corral, and the tack room is open. And have him tell Esperanza I need my hunting boots and rifle, the .30-40 Krag with the scope. Have him tell her I may be gone for quite a while on this one. Got all that?"

"Yes, sir."

Horse got his jacket and went out the door into the purple desert twilight. He headed for his cruiser at a run. His search for the critical evidence in the house of three murders case would have to wait. "It would be nice," he thought, "if I could deal with one thing at a time. But that's never the way this job works." He was going over ninety by the time he passed the Smoke Tree Airport.

He keyed his mike.

"Dispatch."

"Fred, one more thing. Send a deputy to Vidal Junction to take a statement from the supervisor at the inspection station. Have him stop on his way back where he sees my unit. I'll be somewhere close by."

"Got it, Horse."

"I'm already past five-mile, and I'll be past the Southern California Gas compressor station in a few minutes. Once I get over Monument Pass, I'll be out of radio contact for quite a while. If there's anything else I need to know, call the inspection station and have them give the message to our deputy."

"Will do."

By the time Horse reached the abandoned car, darkness had fallen. The Highway Patrolman, Brandon Hicks, was waiting for him beside the red '55 Chevrolet. The driver-side door was open. There were no keys in the ignition. Hicks had already run the plates and had the name, address, and driver's license information of the owner of the car. The license described Harvey Vickers, twenty-eight years old, brown hair, blue eyes, 5' 8", one hundred and ninety pounds. He was from Parker, Arizona.

Horse said, "Brandon, what do you say we find out why Mr. Vickers didn't want to open his trunk?" The patrolman got a tool from his car. Horse retrieved a flashlight from his cruiser and held it while Hicks popped the trunk.

There was a dead woman inside. She was on her back. Her vacant eyes seemed to reflect an aching sense of terror, loss, and regret that went straight to Horse's heart. He suddenly wanted very much to bring Harvey Vickers in if it had indeed been Vickers driving the car.

"My guess is that would be the missus or a girlfriend."

"I think it's the missus. She's wearing a wedding ring."

Horse walked around the car, shining his light on the ground. Several times he knelt down to look at something. Then he walked up and down the road, tracing the flashlight beam from the shoulder into the desert. The light cast filigreed shadows under the creosote bushes beside the road. Puzzled, he turned and walked back to the car.

At the car, he crossed the highway and examined the shoulder on the other side, stopping at one point to point his light out into the desert. He returned to the car once again, where Hicks stood watching him.

"This is confusing. He walked around the car a few times. Looks like he kicked it too."

"Really? You can tell that just by looking at the dirt?"

"Sure. Come here. I'll show you."

Horse lead the patrolman around to the passenger side of the car. He bent down and directed his flashlight to a spot in the dirt.

"See that divot right there?"

"Yeah, I think so. I see something, anyway."

"That's where he pivoted as he pushed off to kick the door. You can also tell he's right-handed because he pivoted on his left foot."

"That's amazing, Lieutenant. You can tell all that just by looking at the ground?"

"Yeah, well, there is one other thing."

"What's that?"

Horse moved the beam to the lower part of the passenger-side door.

"There's also the big footprint he left on the car door."

Hicks laughed.

"Hey, you really had me going there."

"Sorry, couldn't resist. But I do think the man was drunk."

Hicks laughed again. "Don't tell me: You found an empty bottle under the car."

"No, but he fell down when he kicked the car."

Horse moved the flashlight.

"If you look closely, you can see he lost his balance and landed over there. See? That's where he put out his hand to catch himself."

"And that tells you he was drunk?"

"Not just that. I think he was disoriented. When he got up, he walked across the road and headed west."

"But I don't see how that tells you he was drunk."

"It doesn't, positively. But I'm assuming he would want to head for the river since he's going to need water, but he went the other way. Anyone from Parker has to know the river is east of Highway 95. And one last thing: there was still a little daylight when he left the car. Even John Wayne knows you're heading west when you're walking into the setting sun."

"Got it. So, how do we catch this guy?"

"We don't. Not tonight anyway. We know he's got a gun, and we know he's a killer. He's not afraid to shoot people, so there's no point in walking into the desert with flashlights. That's like holding up a sign that says, 'Shoot me!' I've got some deputies on the way. They're bringing horses. We'll track him in the morning."

"Okay. I'm going back on patrol."

"Do me a favor?"

"Sure."

"My radio won't reach Smoke Tree from here. Too many mountains. When you reach Vidal, get on the phone and call my dispatcher. Tell him I need the coroner out here. And a tow truck."

Horse handed him a card. "Here's the office number."

"Will do, Lieutenant."

"And one more thing. Call the Parker substation of the Yuma County Sheriff's Department. Tell them what we found and tell them they might want to check at the address on this guy's license. There might be evidence there."

"Got it. Talk to you later."

Not long after the patrolman left, Horse's deputy from Smoke Tree flashed his brights as he went by on his way to Vidal.

* * *

It was another hour before his deputies showed up, towing trailers behind their pickups. Horse directed them to a spot farther down the highway where they could drive off the road without getting stuck. Then he led them to an area he had picked out, well off the west side of the highway, inside a circle of creosote bushes.

The deputies unloaded the horses, hobbled them, and set out food and water. Once that was done, Horse explained that they had an armed killer wandering around on foot in the desert.

"No point in going after him tonight. That could be a disaster. We'll ride him down tomorrow. Andy, drive north to where the road comes out of Monument Pass. Stop any cars coming this way and turn them around. Tell them what has happened and explain that it's not safe to be out here tonight. We don't want this clown shooting someone to get a car. Tell them the road will be open in the morning. And watch for the coroner's car and the ambulance. When they come by, tell them to look for my cruiser."

"Jim, you go down the road and stop just short of Vidal Junction and turn people around there."

The tow truck showed up next. Horse told the driver to stand by until the coroner got there.

The coroner drove up a half-hour later. Horse led him to the body and stood back to let him make his examination.

"Woman's been strangled. Someone beat her up real bad before he killed her."

While they were talking, the ambulance arrived. The crew put the woman in a body bag and headed for the funeral home in Smoke Tree. The coroner drove off shortly after the ambulance left. Horse had the tow truck take the car to the inspection station at Vidal Junction and leave it there with instructions for them to hold it until they either heard from Horse or someone showed up from the Yuma County Sheriff's Department.

Shortly after the tow truck departed, a sheriff's department vehicle stopped on its way back from Vidal. Horse walked over to the unit. Stuart Atkins was driving.

"Evening Stuart. What did you find out?"

"The guy who was shot is going to be okay. Don't know where the shooter was aiming, but he hit the inspector in the collarbone. Broke it. He's at the hospital in Parker. I drove over and interviewed him there."

"Did he give you a good description of the guy who shot him?"

"Real good." Stuart picked up a notepad off the seat. "Caucasian, mid to late twenties, medium height, overweight. Medium-length, brown hair."

"Did he remember an eye color?"

"Yeah. This guy will make a great witness. Said the shooter's eyes were light blue or maybe gray."

"Okay. That fits the description the highway patrolman got when he ran the driver's license for the registered owner of the car. Good job, Stuart. Write that up and drop it on my desk before you go home."

"Yes, sir, will do. Night, Lieutenant."

"Night."

The deputy drove away. There were no cars on the highway. It was very quiet. Gusts of wind began to whip the creosote bushes and scatter sand across the highway. Desert smells of dust and sage, and creosote came in on the wind. In the middle of the vast desert, far from ambient light, the sky was so dense with stars that there seemed to be little separation between them. The star-filled canopy seemed to bleed into the earth on every side.

He suddenly remembered he and Esperanza had planned to drive to Boulder City for the Smoke Tree football game that evening. After the game, they had planned to go to Las Vegas for dinner and a late show before spending the night. Another date broken. He knew Esperanza would understand. Fortunately, Horse had married a woman who accepted the demands of his job

Horse scouted around for some match weed, then scrounged up some white bursage and creosote to build a fire. By the time he got the small fire going, it was colder, and the smell of the desert changed with the dropping temperature. He got his jacket out of the car and began to gather more creosote sticks for his fire. It took almost an hour to get together a decent pile.

For some reason, he suddenly remembered his father would have called the pile of sticks he had rounded up "widow-woman wood." He realized again how much he missed that good man, taken from his family by the Second World War when Horse was only fourteen years old. His father had died in France, making Horse's *Abuela* one of many gold star mothers in Smoke Tree and leaving Horse's mother to raise him, his younger brother Holguin and his younger sister Benicia on her own. Not a day went by that Horse didn't miss his dad. In fact, he often carried on conversations with him when he was trying to think his way through difficult cases.

He checked the horses and made sure they were okay. Once he was sure they were ready for the night, Horse sat cross-legged in front of his small fire and pondered the sorry state of humanity in general. He could not get the look of sorrow and terror on the dead woman's face out of his mind.

★ ★ ★

Some people are born jerks for no apparent reason. They can be raised in fortunate circumstances by loving and supportive parents. They can have access to opportunity after opportunity that should make them turn out to be good people, but despite all their benefits, they are jerks from childhood. Harvey Vickers was one of those jerks.

When Harvey woke up, he was in the middle of the desert. The first thing he was aware of was the cold. He was wearing a long-sleeved dress shirt, what he called his "go-to-Vegas shirt," and slacks and loafers. He turned his head side to side to find his jacket but didn't see it.

That's when he realized he was lying in the dirt. He sat up and looked around. Bad move! His head began to spin. He tilted onto his side and threw up. He realized he was vomiting on his shirt, but he didn't care. His head hurt too much to change position. When he was done throwing up, he didn't even move out of his own mess. He simply slumped to the ground and fell asleep again despite the cold.

★ ★ ★

When Harvey woke again, it was even colder. His head was pounding, and he was very thirsty. *"I'd kill for a beer,"* he thought.

At the word "kill," it all came flooding back. He'd killed Rose Lynne! Well, what the hell, she deserved it, the whiny bitch!

He sat up again. There was vomit on his shirt but none on the pocket where he kept his cigarettes. He fished them out and stuck one in his mouth. He reached in his pocket for his lighter. It wasn't there. He stood up. His head felt like it was going to come off. He was dizzy, but he had to find that lighter! He really, really needed a smoke. He patted all his pockets. No luck. That's when he realized it was in his jacket pocket, and his jacket was in the car.

And where was his car? Damn thing was always crapping out on him! And it always needed gas, too. He couldn't remember the last time he'd filled it up. He remembered the car sputtering to a stop but couldn't remember if he'd got it off the road.

He remembered killing Rose Lynne. Strangled her, he recalled with almost visceral satisfaction, but not before he'd smacked her around for a while. Thinking about the panicked look in her eyes and her grunts of pain as he pummeled her made him feel better for a minute. That'd teach her to nag him about his drinking. A man should be able to have a drink or two in his own house.

But what had happened in between killing her and the car stopping? He sat back down and tried to remember. He wished he had a beer and a cigarette. That would help.

Suddenly, he saw himself hauling his worthless wife's sorry carcass down the back porch steps and stuffing her into the trunk. Lord, he was lucky the neighbors hadn't seen that! Then he remembered going back into the house and opening another bottle. Well, why not? At least there was no Rose Lynne to complain anymore.

He remembered drinking straight from the bottle and wondering what to do next. That's when he decided to go ahead and go to Vegas. That's what had started their whole argument in the first place. Another thing he wouldn't have to hear Rose Lynne bitch about unless she could get out of that trunk. He didn't think that was likely.

He recalled taking a shower. Only fell down once while he was doing it, too. Then he put on his Vegas shirt and Vegas loafers. *Really should've dried off first,* he thought. But he had been in a hurry. He pulled up his pants leg. Yep! Forgot his socks too.

Well, a guy couldn't remember everything. But at least he remembered his gun. Never could tell what might happen in Vegas. When he'd pulled open the drawer to get his gun, that's when he'd had the brilliant idea. He'd bury Rose Lynne in the desert outside Las Vegas. It would be perfect. It would be dark when he got there, so no one would see him. And even if someone did find her body someday, they'd just think it was another mob killing. Hell, he had heard those mafia guys murdered people all the time and buried the bodies in the desert!

Once he'd buried Rose Lynne, he'd spend the night in Vegas and drive home on Saturday. When he got there, he would clean up the house and get rid of any evidence. Then he'd call Rose Lynne's mom and ask if she'd seen her daughter, explaining he'd come home to an empty house. He'd call the sheriff's department and report her missing. Great plan. No reason why it wouldn't work.

He recalled leaving Parker and driving over the Colorado River into California. Then he came to the California Agricultural Inspection Station. And that's when everything went wrong. He thought they would just wave him through. They always did.

He told them he didn't have any fruits or vegetables, but that idiot of an inspector told him to pull over beside the station and open his trunk. Well, that would have been just crazy! The guy would've seen Rose Lynne's body. He had no choice but to shoot him! So, it was the inspector's fault! None of this would have happened if he hadn't told Harvey to pull over. He would've been in Vegas by now, done with burying Rose Lynne and looking for a hot craps table at the Horseshoe Club. And speaking of burying people, he suddenly realized he'd forgot to bring a shovel. But it had been smart to bring his gun, so he hadn't done everything wrong.

So, no car, no jacket, no cigarette lighter, no water. Ah, what the hell? He would just walk until he got to the Colorado River. Plenty of water there.

He started walking, stumbling through the shallow, sandy wash, cursing the desert. The sky was full of stars, but it was still hard to see. He kept scanning the sky, hoping a big moon would rise. He walked on and on, but still no moon. Maybe there wasn't going to be a moon tonight.

His feet started to hurt. Small rocks and bits of gravel were sneaking over the sides of his loafers, and with no socks between the debris and his feet, it was getting damned uncomfortable. But he was determined to get to the river, no matter how badly his feet hurt, so he kept plodding onward, cursing Rose Lynne for making him kill her, cursing the agricultural inspector for getting shot. Christ! Would he never catch a break?

★ ★ ★

His life had not always been like this. When he was younger, things had been good. He was a late-in-life baby. Dalton and Wanda Vickers had long since resigned themselves to being childless when one of his old man's sperm made a lucky strike. Voilà! Harvey appeared. They were so delighted to have him that they began spoiling him the moment he was born. Especially his mother. As far as Wanda was concerned, Harvey was perfect in every way, no matter what he did.

But Dalton was not as blind to his son's faults. Even before grade school, Dalton knew something was amiss. Harvey liked to play with matches and torment the family dog, and once he reached puberty, he really hit his stride! He was always in trouble at school and with the neighbors, especially the Stouts, the ones who accused Harvey of trying to pull their seven-year-old's panties down in the garage one afternoon. The same people accused him of dousing their cat with gasoline and setting it on fire. Fortunately for Harvey, his mother refused to believe any of it. She always took his side, and Dalton soon realized that he had better do the same if he wanted to be at peace with his wife.

The way Harvey saw it, the good thing was not only was his dad a really old guy with a faulty ticker, but he was also the owner of a very prosperous grocery store. So when Harvey graduated from Phoenix Union High School in 1950, he was sure he would soon inherit the family business. Of course, there was the matter of the Korean War, but his father knew someone who knew someone. Soon enough, Harvey was classified 4-F because of a non-existent medical condition diagnosed by a respected doctor in Phoenix.

Harvey went to work at the family store, safe from the war and other misfortunes. But his father quickly realized that Harvey was no help. Dalton could not even leave him alone at the store because the kid was prone to tapping the register and then blaming the theft on others. Dalton had fired a good employee before he'd figured that one out.

When Harvey graduated, Dalton was seventy years old. His heart condition was worsening. He had hoped to have

Harvey run the store so he could at least slow down. But when he realized how unreliable and dishonest his son really was, he decided to sell out. He didn't tell anyone of his decision: not Harvey and certainly not his wife.

Dalton quietly negotiated a good deal with an expanding Arizona supermarket chain. The first Wanda knew about it was when Dalton came home and put a "for sale" sign in the yard. She screamed bloody murder, but for once, Dalton refused to back down. He told Wanda she could either come with him to Vermont to spend their golden years together or live in poverty with her untrustworthy son in Phoenix.

Wanda folded. They sold the house. She and Dalton moved back to Vermont, where they had come from all those long years ago. They both agreed they wouldn't miss the Phoenix summers, and time had papered over the reality of the Vermont winters. They only chose to remember the white Christmases of childhood, with carolers on the porch and a big fire in the fireplace.

Dalton made it quite clear to Harvey that he was not coming along. But he did his son one favor, even though the favor to Harvey was a disservice to a long-time friend. Dalton wrote a letter of recommendation to the owner of a grocery store in Parker. Dalton praised the managerial skills of his son, touting him as perfect assistant manager material. Dalton hoped that he would be long gone by the time the truth came out. When Dalton and Wanda left for Vermont, Harvey headed for Parker with his letter of recommendation in a sealed envelope. On the strength of his father's praise, he was hired.

Walking and thinking about the past soon wore Harvey out. He was cold and tired. He scouted out a place next to a cutbank in a wash where lots of sand and gravel had accumulated. He lay down on his side and curled into a fetal position. Within minutes, he was asleep for the third time since he had walked into the desert.

★ ★ ★

After an hour, Horse nodded off under a star-filled sky into which the moon had not yet risen. Every time the cold wind gusted, he woke up, checked his watch, and put a few more sticks on his fire.

At ten o'clock, he drove down the road toward Smoke Tree. He spotted Andy's pickup across the road from a "curves ahead" highway sign riddled with bullet holes like so many road signs in the desert. Horse parked on the shoulder and walked across the highway.

"Evenin', Andy."

"Evening, Lieutenant. I turned back all four cars that came by after the ambulance and the coroner."

"Good. Here's what I want you to do now. Drive back to the horses and sleep until two o'clock. Then go and take Jim's place. Tell him to go back to the horses and get some sleep.

First light will be about 5:45. At five o'clock, get us some food and coffee at the diner in Vidal. Here's a twenty. Hang onto the receipt, so I can get reimbursed. Bring the food back to where Jim and the horses are. I'll meet you there. As soon as we eat, we'll start after this guy."

"Okay, Lieutenant. See you in the morning."

Horse stood beside the road and watched Andy's lights recede southward on 95. Before long, it was as if he had never been there. There were no lights anywhere. Horse realized this was what this land had been like when it was ruled by Spain and later by Mexico. A place of almost total emptiness, except for a few widely-scattered Chemehuevi clawing an existence out of the unyielding and unforgiving land.

After a while, Horse returned to his cruiser to watch for oncoming cars.

DAY TWO

When Harvey woke for the third time, he was colder and thirstier but stone-cold sober. He got wearily to his feet and headed up the wash rising gradually in front of him. He walked for a long time before noticing more light in the sky than earlier. He thought it must be false dawn. He scanned the sky for some sign of the rising sun.

Suddenly, he realized the light was coming from behind him. He turned around and stared open-mouthed at the third-quarter moon. The moon had risen behind him while he slept and was well above the horizon. Behind him!

Harvey had no idea how to tell time by the moon's phases, but he knew the damn thing came up in the east. All this time, he had been walking the wrong direction! He scrambled up over the cut bank and looked around.

How had he started off the wrong direction? He tried to recreate the events after his stupid car quit on him. He'd pulled the keys out of the ignition and got out. He remembered walking around the car. Then he lost his temper and kicked the damn thing as hard as he could, kicked it so hard he lost his balance and fell down. Then he got up and started walking.

That was it! He could remember his Vegas shoes clicking on the asphalt. Good, God! He'd been so drunk he'd crossed the road and started off the wrong way! Now that he was sober, he began to think clearly. Someone at the inspection station would have called the cops. After all, he'd shot someone. So the police must have found his car by now. Since they knew he shot the inspector to keep him from looking in the trunk, they would have pried it open. That meant they had found Rose Lynne.

He doubted they'd come out into the desert looking for him in the dark. No, they'd wait until daylight. So, he had to do two things. He had to elude his pursuers, and he had to get to the river for water. He had no idea how long it was until sunup, but he knew he had to get moving.

First things first. He'd made no attempt to cover his tracks, so even though it probably wasn't easy to track someone through the desert, he would have to make it harder if he wanted to get away. He turned and started walking north.

★ ★ ★

He walked north and crossed several washes before he found what he was looking for. It was a wide expanse of rocks that sloped off to the east. He'd seen this kind of stuff out in the desert before. The stones were round and smooth, packed so tightly together that they made an almost-even surface.

He stood and thought for a while, then headed west again. After a few hundred yards, he stepped off the desert pavement and into the wash to the south. He stepped hard and pushed off hard with each step until he got across the wash to some rocky ground. Then he walked carefully backward through the tracks he's made until he got back to the pavement. When he reached it, he turned east. "There!" he thought. "Figure that out. And then let's see you try to track me over this."

★ ★ ★

In the pre-dawn, Horse and his deputies gathered at the horse trailers for breakfast. As they ate and drank their coffee, they discussed the coming search.

"So, our guy's headed west?"

"Looks like."

"What's out there, Lieutenant?"

"Not much. If he keeps going west, he'll bump into the Stepladder Mountains in fifteen miles. No water out there. If he turns southwest, he'll hit the Mopah range in about the same distance. No water there either. If he turns northwest, he'll be walking toward the Old Woman Mountains. There's water there, but those mountains are a long, long way away."

"What do you think he'll do?"

"Hard to guess. As I explained to the highway patrolman before you guys got here, this man was very drunk. So drunk he walked off to the west where there's no water. Where there's not much of anything. My guess is, he thought he was walking toward the river if he was thinking at all.

Now, he may have walked far enough to sober up, or he may have laid down in a sandy wash and slept it off. Either way, if he was awake after midnight when the third quarter moon rose up behind him, he should have realized he was going the wrong way. If he did, maybe he turned around or at least turned north or south. Or maybe he didn't. Maybe he just kept going.

Since we have no way of knowing what he was thinking last night or is thinking now, we'll just have to track him to find out what he did and where he's gone.

Since we know for sure he started west, I'm not comfortable leaving the horses and vehicles here unattended. Jim, I want you to stay here until Andy and I come for you. Every fifteen minutes, climb up in the back of your truck and glass the area in both directions. You might catch him on his way back."

Horse and Andy saddled their mounts. The leather creaked in the cold air when they swung into their saddles. The sun was not yet up. When they had been riding for a few minutes, it rose above the rim of the Chemehuevi Mountains behind them. The low angle of the light cast their elongated shadows far ahead of them, giving them the appearance of mythological minotaurs riding off in search of some fabled destiny. As it rose, the sun etched sharp patterns of light and shadow on the distant Stepladder Mountains, making them look like brown paper crumpled and cast aside. And like something created unintentionally but created nonetheless, they beckoned the two men on horseback, moving ahead of the sun.

Horse did the tracking. From what sign he could find, it seemed clear that the man was making no attempt at evasion. But for all that, it was slow going. It is no simple task to track a person across desert terrain.

Vickers' trail moved in a meandering line in and out of washes. The man was generally, but not always, moving to the west. In places where he had left the sandy washes and moved onto rocky ground, his trail disappeared. Whenever it did, Horse had Andy hold Canyon while casting in increasingly wide arcs until he picked up the track again.

They hadn't been searching too long before Horse found the place where Vickers had stopped and been sick. Red ants were already at work on the mess he had left behind. It was unclear whether the man had rested in the spot for a significant amount of time, but Horse could tell he had laid down.

The tracks from where he had been sick led more or less to the west. There still seemed to be no attempt at evasion. Vickers must have still been drunk.

When Horse returned from one of his time-consuming searches to relocate a trail that had disappeared in rocky terrain, Andy had a question.

"Lieutenant, you know all about this desert. Explain something to me."

"What's that?"

"Why are these creosote bushes so much taller than the ones around Smoke Tree?"

"Because this is where the Colorado Desert and Mojave Desert come together. This is the northernmost edge of the Colorado Desert, and it gets some of the monsoon rains that come up from the Sea of Cortez in August and early September. But those rains never reach Smoke Tree. That's why the creosote bushes here are taller. The higher we get, the more rain in August, and the taller they'll be. Some of them will get up to nine feet or so."

"Doesn't make looking for this guy any easier, does it?"

"No, it doesn't."

They moved on. Small, gray birds began to follow them, flitting from bush to bush. When Canyon lifted his tail, Horse looked back to see birds contesting the animal's droppings. The birds were not, however, the gray birds. They were black-throated sparrows and house finches. Horse wondered where they had appeared from so suddenly.

As they moved closer to the Stepladders, the Mopahs rotated farther away from them to the south. The Old Woman Mountains, however, were so far to the north that their position seemed to remain unchanged.

★ ★ ★

Around ten o'clock, Horse found the spot where Vickers had stopped again. He had stopped next to the cutbank on the south side of the wash and rested. Then he had moved out again. He must have sobered up because his track did not wander as much. That was a blessing. Horse didn't have to dismount as often to pick up his trail.

The farther west they moved, the deeper the washes became as the land inclined toward the mountains that were the source of countless flash floods. As the washes deepened, Horse began to see stunted desert willows, many bearing the unwanted burden of parasitic mistletoe. Small, struggling cat-claw acacia began to appear, mixed in with the rounded forms of cheesebush. Canyon tossed his head in annoyance when he caught the sickly odor of those pungent shrubs.

An hour later, Horse found one more resting place. Once again, Vickers had located a sandy spot before lying down. His tracks showed he had moved west for some distance after standing, but then had stopped and walked in a little circle.

Horse stood looking at the tracks.

"This is interesting. Step down and come over here."

He waited while Andy dismounted.

"I think we've come to where our man realized he'd been walking away from the river. You can see where his tracks turn perpendicular to the wash, and he moves off to the north. His strides get longer, too. He's moving like a man with a purpose. For the first time since we've been tracking him, he's going in a straight line. I think our job is about to get harder."

"Why's that?"

"Because I think he was entirely sober by the time he got up from that last resting spot. Sober and starting to think. Starting to think someone might come looking for him. So now he's going to try to lose us."

"So why'd he go north instead of east?"

"Once he realized he'd been going the wrong way, he didn't want to double back and run into anyone who might be coming after him."

"So, how does he intend to lose us?"

"He's looking for something in particular. We'll know when he finds it."

Another hour later, Vickers' tracks disappeared. Horse and Andy had just come out of one of the many small washes onto a broad, flat rise that spread east and west. They found no trail on the other side when they crossed the rise.

Horse had Andy hold Canyon while he cast increasingly wider arcs on both sides of the rise. Andy saw him turn west on the rise for a few hundred yards and then turn south back into the wash. When he reached the far side of the shallow wash, he made a few short arcs before returning to Andy.

"Our fugitive knows something about the desert. He's not just a town guy. Maybe hunts a bit. He was looking for a place just like this. He's smart but not as smart as he thinks."

"Why is this place so special?"

"This stuff we're standing on is called desert pavement. Smooth, round rocks compressed into the soil. It's almost like a road. He was crossing all those washes looking for this. He knew he'd be hard to track once he found a place like this."

"Well, that is smart. But why isn't he as smart as he thinks?"

"Because I don't think it occurred to him we'd know why he'd changed direction. He probably thought we'd waste a lot of time trying to figure out which way he went. That's why he went a few hundred yards up that way and then turned and walked across the wash to the rocky ground on the other side."

"So he went south?"

"He wants us to think he did. But he made a couple of amateur mistakes. First, he stepped down and pushed off extra hard so I'd be sure to find his tracks. That made it way too obvious. Then, when he got to the other side, he walked backward through his tracks and got back on the pavement. He thinks we'll waste a lot of time trying to figure out which way he went."

"And we're not going to?"

"No. There's no doubt in my mind he turned east once he got done backtracking. But it's still going to slow us down a bit. We can't be one hundred percent sure he will stay on this until it runs out, so we'll have to keep checking either side of the rocks to make sure he doesn't move north or south again."

They moved again. Occasionally, a black-tailed jackrabbit broke cover ahead of them and sprinted away until it was lost from sight. In a few hundred yards, another would break cover and bound off into the distance. Horse was never sure whether it was the same rabbit over and over or a different one each time. Then, they rode a long way without seeing any jackrabbits. Horse looked skyward. Two golden eagles soared in opposing circles overhead, riding the thermals. When predators are aloft, jackrabbits do not break cover.

High above the eagles, he saw buzzards floating, their dihedral wings outstretched as they manipulated the air around them to stay aloft. Waiting for the eagles to catch something, no doubt, and perhaps leave some remnant behind after they fed.

Horse never saw buzzards in the sky without wondering what they saw up there. Did everything that walked or crawled look like a potential meal? They sometimes rose so high on the thermals they disappeared to the naked eye. What then? Surely they were too high to spot anything to eat. Horse suspected they soared so high just for its joy, just because they could.

Andy and Horse proceeded slowly for almost an hour before Horse dismounted again.

"First mistake. He's getting tired and careless. He stumbled and kicked one of the rocks loose. See here? He might have got away with it if he'd put it back, but he left it lying here with the dirty side up."

★ ★ ★

As Harvey moved east over the desert pavement, he tried to pick up the pace a bit, even though his feet were killing him. He was very thirsty. As he moved, he began to hatch a plan. If he could just get to Lake Havasu, he could make his way south, staying close enough to the lake to get water when he needed it. He could skirt around Parker Dam and make for town if he stayed near the shoreline.

There was something there he really wanted to do: He had some business to attend to with his mother-in-law! What the hell, in for a penny, in for a pound, right? His whole plan had blown up because of the agricultural inspector. If they caught him, he was going to jail anyway. Might as well settle a score first.

As he walked into the dawn of a new day, he thought back to his life when he'd first arrived in Parker, gone to work for Mr. Bondurant, and met Rose Lynne.

Harvey kept his nose clean at work after remembering the problems he had gone through at his father's store. He was determined to gain Mr. Bondurant's confidence. He rented a cheap apartment and managed to live within his means. After two years, he was promoted to the assistant manager's job, and as Mr. Bondurant relied on him more, Harvey began to run the store on his own at times. That allowed him to take items out the back door and pick up some extra cash. He was always careful not to take too much.

After work was another story. It didn't take him long to fall in with a bad crowd. His best friend was Kendrick Fahrnam, the town tough. Harvey had gone out of his way to make friends with the guy. A clever suck-up, Harvey was smart enough to know that no one would mess with him if he hung around with the baddest guy in town.

The problem was that Kendrick drank heavily. To be his pal, Harvey was soon slugging it down too. Still, although he skated around the edge of the serious-trouble pond while tagging along with Kendrick and his friends, he never actually fell in. He had been surprised at how much he had come to enjoy life in such a hick town.

Toward the end of his first year as assistant manager, Rose Lynne Spartan, a recent graduate of Parker High School, applied for a job at the market. Mr. Bondurant hired her.

Harvey certainly had no complaint. Rose Lynne was a very pretty girl. Also, she was very impressed with Harvey, and he was flattered. It wasn't long before they were dating. The only problem was Rose Lynne's mother, Pearl Spartan. She was not at all taken with Harvey Vickers. It hadn't taken her long to figure out what kind of person existed just below that polite but smug exterior, and it wasn't the kind of person she wanted her daughter to get tangled up with.

But Rose Lynne was eighteen and had a mind of her own. Within a year, Rose Lynne was Mrs. Vickers. While Pearl was less than pleased, there was nothing she could do about it. She had hoped the newlyweds would move in with her so she could keep an eye on Harvey. But Harvey wanted no part of that. He and Rose Lynne moved into his tiny apartment.

Between the two of them, they made a decent living. Within two years, they had saved enough to make a down payment on a small, wood-frame house. When they moved into their modest home, Harvey and Rose Lynne Vickers began to live a scaled-down version of the American Dream.

Once they had their own house, Rose Lynne wanted to start a family. But after three years of marriage, Rose Lynne was still not in a family way. Although he never admitted it to Rose Lynne, Harvey was pretty sure he was the problem.

After all, it had taken his old man thirty years to get his mom pregnant.

Harvey wasn't heartbroken about their failure to conceive. He liked the double income, and he wasn't all that crazy about having some greedy little crumb snatcher enter the picture. He had his house, a pretty little wife, and he was still good friends with Kendrick.

But his friendship with Kendrick caused friction between them. Rose Lynne didn't like him. She thought he was crude, lewd, and rude, and she didn't like the guy's eyes crawling all over her body. But Harvey didn't seem to notice. Or maybe he just didn't care what she thought. To his way of thinking, he was the master of the house and his little world and could do what he damn well pleased.

Rose Lynne was a quiet little girl. Her idea of a nice evening was sitting around reading a book or listening to a radio program. Sure, she had gone partying with Harvey in the past, but everyone did those things while dating. But she didn't want to do them once they were married. And another thing: she hated cigarette smoke. Although she had never complained while they were courting, she began to nag Harvey to quit once they were married.

By 1960, after six years of marriage, their lives had settled into a routine of more or less constant bickering. Harvey was drinking too much and still hanging around with Kendrick. And Rose Lynne had found a hobby of her own: eating. Every time she and Harvey had one of their increasingly loud arguments and he stormed out to pal around with Kendrick, Rose Lynne drove to her mother's house and consoled herself with cakes and cookies and half-gallons of pralines and cream. Pearl was more than happy to supply the sweets in return for being able to bad-mouth Harvey for a few hours. The more Rose Lynne and Harvey argued, the more she packed on the pounds. The shapely girl he had married began to puff up in a most unappealing manner.

Harvey had also taken to gambling. Whenever they managed to save up a little money, he went off to Las Vegas and blew it all on craps or slots. The first few times, he took her along, but Rose Lynne hated casinos. They were loud and so full of cigarette smoke she could hardly breathe. Not only that, she got so mad watching him lose two months' savings in a few hours that she could hardly stand it.

And that's what had led to their final, fatal argument. Harvey wanted to head to Las Vegas on Friday. He arranged to get off work at noon to get a head start. But Rose Lynne didn't want him to go. She had managed to squirrel away a couple of hundred dollars, and she knew he would not quit gambling until he lost it all. They argued, and as they did, Harvey started drinking. Soon she was screaming in frustration. The more she screamed, the more he drank.

By three o'clock, he was pretty much in the bag but more determined than ever to hit the tables. When he headed for the door, she tried to stop him. Soon, he was bouncing her off the walls and the furniture. And that's when she said it.

"Is this how you prove you're a man? Beat up your wife? Because you sure can't get her pregnant, can you? Mother says none of the women in our family ever had trouble conceiving, so it must be you, Mr. Big Man."

That's when Harvey started pounding her as hard as he could. He didn't stop until she quit moving. Just to be sure, he wrapped his hands around her neck and squeezed for a long time.

Now there was no doubt in his mind it had all been Pearl's fault! She must have been poisoning Rose Lynne against him for years before Rose Lynne let slip the slur on his potency. Straight from Pearl's lips, no doubt. Well, Harvey wasn't going to let her get away with it. No way! She had ruined Harvey's life by making him kill Rose Lynne. He was going to make her pay. Once again, he congratulated himself on his foresight in bringing his gun.

He kept moving through the desert.

★ ★ ★

A half-hour later, the rock-covered plain bled into sandy desert. While he tried to walk carefully through the creosote bushes, he knew someone who could track well could probably follow if they were good enough to have tracked him to this point. But he had a solution in mind for that problem.

It took him another half hour to get to Highway 95. He stood on the shoulder for a long time, looking both directions and listening for vehicles. When he was sure nothing was coming, he moved out onto the highway and ran south down the middle of the road until he couldn't run any farther. He slowed to a walk and kept going until he was opposite a place where the ground was rocky on the other side of the road.

He walked across the shoulder and onto the rocky ground. He scouted around until he found a big branch on one of the creosotes. He broke it off, went back to the shoulder, and brushed out his tracks, walking backward until he got onto the rocky ground again.

Satisfied, he set off to the southeast.

★ ★ ★

Even though Horse was sure he knew where Vickers was headed, he didn't want to be overconfident. He continually moved from one side to the other of the forty-yard-wide stretch of desert pavement. This slowed his progress, but he wanted to be sure the man hadn't veered off and moved north or south.

When the broad plain of tightly-knit, embedded rocks dwindled to an end, Horse handed Canyon's reins to Andy and proceeded on foot. It looked as though Vickers had tried to move toward the highway without leaving any trace; however, he wasn't that hard to follow.

But when Vickers reached the highway, he had done something clever. Instead of simply crossing and continuing on his way, he had obviously walked on the highway where he could not be tracked. That meant the man was aware he was being followed.

Horse came back across the highway to where Andy was waiting.

"Instead of just crossing the road, he walked on the highway here. There's really no way to tell which way he went, but my gut tells me he went south. South is home. South is where he might have a friend who would help him. South is a lot of things that north isn't.

But just to be sure, I'm going to ride a half-mile or so up the road and see if I can pick up his tracks on the east side of the road. I think that'll be far enough. No matter which direction he went, I doubt he'd stay out on the road much farther than that. Too much of a chance of being spotted. If I don't find his trail, I'll check down the west side of the road all the way back, then cross over and start checking to the south.

I want you to stay on the west side of the highway and ride back toward the horse trailers. Keep an eye on the ground for any sign Vickers cut back to the west.

If you find anything, stop and wait for me. If you don't find anything by the time you get back to the horse trailers, have Jim saddle up. Here's the keys to my unit. In the trunk, you'll find a case of C-rations. Open the case and bring us six meals. Anything but ham and lima beans. And get some extra water. When you get done, lock my shotgun in the trunk. Be real embarrassing for the substation commander to have his shotgun stolen. Lock everything else up tight and cross over to the east side of the road and wait for me."

Horse led Canyon across the highway and mounted up. He rode slowly north, paralleling 95 and looking for any evidence Vickers had gone that way. After about a half-mile, he was satisfied the man had not. Horse crossed the highway and moved south until he was opposite his starting point. He dismounted and led Canyon on foot while he examined the shoulder. In less than a mile, he found what he had been looking for.

Boy's watched too many western movies, Horse thought as he read the story written in the dirt. It was easy to see Vickers had tried to erase his tracks by walking backward and brushing the ground. He might as well have drawn a big arrow pointing to the east and written, "I went that way." Horse even found the creosote branch Vickers had discarded when he was done. Horse pulled a red bandana from his saddlebags and tied it to a creosote bush so he could find the spot when he returned. Then he set off to meet Andy and Jim.

★ ★ ★

Within half an hour, he brought them to the bandana.

"It looks to me like he's moving southeast. If he kept going that way, he would have hit a fork in this low wash after a while. I'm a little worried about what he did after that. Trampas Wash splits off to the southeast, and Red Rock Wash goes northeast. I'm hoping he took Red Rock. If he did, he'll fetch up against Red Rock Falls. That's a really rugged cliff face. No way he'll be able to get over it. He'll have to come back toward us.

I'll take the center. Andy, you stay about fifty yards to the south, and Jim, you stay about the same distance to my north. I'm going to be face down a lot, so I want the two of you to keep your eyes peeled in front of us. We're probably closing in on him. Stop now and then and scope the area out in front of us. I don't want to stumble on this guy unawares. He has a gun, and he's just dumb enough to use it."

They moved out. The sun was already tilting to the west. Their elongated shadows, which had preceded them to the west in the morning light, now splayed out in front of them as they moved east. The creosote thrashed about in the rising north wind. Even the white bursage was agitated into movement.

As they continued, they began crossing a series of low hills. On the slopes were grayish-green brittlebush, bereft of the glorious yellow flowers they had displayed in the spring. The desiccated stems jutted above the foliage, looking like a rusty framework to which something was supposed to be attached. Zebra-tailed lizards made erratic sprints through the sand, frequently stopping to do frenetic push-ups as they sur-veyed their surroundings for bugs or danger.

They saw desert lavender as the land began to rise to the east toward the Chemehuevi mountains. The amount of catclaw increased, and verdins called from inside the thorny bushes as they rode past. Solitary phainopepla could not be seen, but they heard their up-slurred whistled *hoooeets* and low quirks. A mockingbird serenaded them with a symphony of the songs of other birds.

★ ★ ★

They didn't find the man they were hunting until a little after three o'clock. Horse was surprised at how much ground the guy had covered. Jim Harkness spotted him and rode over to Horse for instructions. They called Andy and sat the horses while deciding what to do next.

"He's on the edge of the wash, just over that low hill. Looks to me like he's about give out."

"I thought we were going to get lucky. Looked like he was going to take the northeast fork, but he's crossing over to the south wash.

Well, let's get off these horses so we don't make such nice targets. We'll walk him down on foot."

They tied the horses and headed for the low hill. They moved carefully between increasing amounts of buckhorn and teddy bear cholla as they climbed.

When they saw Vickers again, he was climbing the raised area that separated Red Rock Wash from Trampas Wash. Horse put the glasses on him. Vickers didn't have a gun in his hand.

"Tell you what. Let's walk a little closer. I don't see the gun, and anyway, we're way out of pistol range."

Vickers never looked back as they walked toward him. He seemed intent on moving toward Trampas Wash. They continued to follow him until he went over the low hill. They went up the hill after him.

"He might turn around. Don't silhouette yourself on top."

When they approached the crest, Horse dropped low for a few steps, then crawled forward. He scanned the desert with his binoculars. Vickers was headed down the other side. He was now moving southeast. Horse didn't know if the man had changed direction on purpose or was just getting disoriented.

Horse dropped back below the crest and motioned his deputies forward.

"I don't think he has any idea we're up here. Let's all go quietly up to the top. Crawl the last few feet. Put your scopes on him while I holler at him, but no matter what he does, don't shoot unless I tell you to."

Both deputies nodded. The three men moved to the crest together. When his deputies had their scopes on the man, Horse cupped his hands and yelled.

"Hey! Hey you!"

Vickers was in the wide wash. He turned around and looked toward the hillside. It was obvious he didn't see them.

"San Bernardino County Sheriff's Department. Get your gun out and throw it as far as you can. Do it now!"

Vickers continued to scan the desert hillside, then suddenly seemed to spot something. He broke to his right and ran in a shuffling scramble to some rocks. He tried to hide behind them and a catclaw bush, but he was not entirely concealed.

Horse let Vickers stay there with his head down. He could see the man shifting his position. Probably trying to get his pistol out of his pants without standing up.

"Come on, Vickers. You've got no way out of this. We have rifles and you have a handgun. Throw it away and stand up."

His arm and then his head appeared above the rocks.

"Andy, has he got a gun in his hand?"

"Yeah. Looks like a small semi-automatic of some kind."

Horse put the glasses on the man again. His weapon looked like a Colt Woodsman, .22 caliber. While he was looking at the gun, he saw a puff of smoke, then he heard the tiny "pop" of a .22.

"Well, hell," said Andy.

"Lieutenant, I've got the crosshairs right on the little pissant. Want me to shoot him?"

"Nah. If you do, we'll have to carry him. He's just lying there. He looks like a kid pretending we can't see him. We've got water and food. He doesn't. We just wait him out. He's not going anywhere that we can't follow."

Horse sat and thought for a few minutes about the two deputies he had with him. Jim Harkness was more experienced but also overweight and seemed a little trigger-happy. Horse had a feeling there would be a lot of walking involved before this problem was solved. A lot of patience would also be required. He thought Andy better suited on both counts.

"Jim, you go on ahead back to town. Andy and I are going to be out here all night. When you get to the station, let the relief dispatcher know what's going on. Have him inform San Bernardino we've had a homicide, and we're tracking a suspect. Make sure he tells them everything is under control and we don't need any help. I don't want a bunch of people stomping around out here. I figure this guy is good for another day at the most, and then we can take him without shooting him.

Also, have him contact the Yuma County substation in Parker and let them know we're closing in on the man who killed his wife and shot the agricultural inspector."

"Got it, boss."

Jim pulled back off the crest and started down the hill to the horses.

Partway down, he turned and called back. "You two be careful out here."

"We will, Jim. It's not as if the guy has a real gun."

Water! It was all he could think about. Cold water from the Colorado River. Tall glasses of water. Glasses filled with water and shaved ice, beaded with moisture. A memory flashed into his mind of the cold, delicious water from Hummingbird Spring back behind Oatman, where he often hunted quail. He remembered how the ice-cold artesian water splashed over the edges of the cement cistern someone had built.

The odd thing was, he no longer wanted a beer. He didn't want a Coke either. Or a milkshake, or even iced tea with a sprig of mint. No. He wanted water. Gallons of water. Lakes of water. Wanted it so badly he'd gladly shoot someone for it.

Bone tired, he sat down and looked back the way he'd come. God, he hated this desert! Ugly, dusty, barren, hostile place! Nothing of use in all this vast and disgusting desolation. And now he was on foot in the middle of it without water!

He knew the people following him couldn't be too far away. The man who had yelled at him to surrender had said, "We have rifles." Maybe the man wasn't alone. But maybe he was. Maybe he was just trying to make Harvey think he had a posse. After all, Harvey had only seen one hat above the edge of the hill. Maybe he should go back and see if whoever it was had built a fire to heat food or keep warm. Maybe he could sneak up on the camp if there was a fire. Shoot the guy or guys. Get their water.

No, it was too far to retrace his steps. He should have thought of it before he started walking. Besides, what if there were five of them or ten? He would end up getting shot. While he sat watching his back trail, he fell asleep.

★ ★ ★

After they finished their meals, Horse explained what he had been concerned about earlier.

"Vickers is moving southeast now. Just what I didn't want him to do. I was hoping he'd go northeast at the fork."

"I remember you said earlier if he went northeast, he'd hit a dead end."

"But there's something else. Somebody lives off in the general direction he's moving. I'm just not sure exactly where."

"Come on, Lieutenant, there's not even a road out there."

"This guy doesn't use roads. Doesn't need them."

"Who in the world would live out there?"

"Joe Medrano. Folks around here, those that have ever seen him, call him 'Chemehuevi Joe.' He's an Indian."

"Lieutenant, I've heard of Mojaves, Navajos, Hopis, and even Hualapais since I've been working out of Smoke Tree substation, but I've never heard of a Chem... Chemi.."

"Chemehuevei."

"Right. Chemehuevi. Where's their reservation?"

"Don't have one. It was taken away from them. And not only that, they're not even recognized by the government as a real tribe anymore."

"You mean he's the last of them?"

"No, there's a couple hundred of them, but they're scattered all to hell and gone now."

"How does that even happen? How do you lose a reservation?"

"I take it you're not a student of the history of the American Indian. They lost it the same way Indians usually lose things. The way the Sioux lost their land in the Black Hills when gold was discovered there. All of a sudden, the treaty the Sioux had signed with the U.S. Government was no good. They got kicked off the land."

"You mean somebody discovered gold? Out here?"

"Nope. Something even better."

"What's better than gold?"

"Water. What used to be the Chemehuevi reservation is now underneath Lake Havasu. The government wanted the Chemehuevi's land for the reservoir when they built Parker Dam."

"So they just took it?"

"Yep. And took away the Chemehuevi's status as a tribe so the tribe couldn't sue to stop the project. The government knew if they were no longer listed as a tribe, they wouldn't have standing in court."

"Good God. Did they have to do all that?"

"Who knows how those yahoos in Washington think? My guess was they were afraid the tribe would hook up with Arizona lawmakers who didn't want the dam built."

"Why did Arizona care?"

"Arizona was afraid California would steal all the water Arizona was entitled to in the Colorado River Compact."

"So what happened?"

"The governor sent a detachment of the Arizona National Guard."

"Come on, Lieutenant, you're making this up."

"Nope. There wasn't even a decent road out here from Phoenix in those days, so the soldiers marched across the desert and hauled a World War One field gun behind a team of horses."

"What did they do when they got to Parker?"

"Remembered they'd forgotten something important."

"What was that?"

"A boat. They had their gun, but they couldn't get it close enough to the dam site without a boat."

"What'd they do?"

"Borrowed one from the Bureau of Reclamation. Somehow got it up to the dam site and threatened to shoot the cannon if construction didn't stop on the project. The government kept on working. The way I heard the story from my father, the soldiers fired a warning shot, and the recoil capsized the boat. They went into the river: boots, uniforms, weapons, and all. They were lucky they didn't drown. When they got out of the river, they packed up and marched back to Phoenix, short one field gun."

"What did the government do?"

"Sent the governor of Arizona a bill for the boat. I heard he tore it up."

"When was this?"

"Nineteen thirty-five. That's when the government took the reservation land and de-listed the tribe. The Chemhuevi just kept right on living where they'd always lived. But the flood gates at Parker Dam were closed in 1940, and the reservoir began to fill up."

"What happened to the Chemehuevi?"

"It was either move or drown. They left. Some went to 29 Palms, some to other places."

"What about Joe?"

"This was the tail end of the Depression. People forget this now, but things were getting bad again. Roosevelt thought he had whipped the Depression, but it was coming back. There were no jobs out here for an Indian. Like a lot of men, Joe hit the rails. Wandered all over the country, working wherever he could find something."

"That must have been hard."

"Must have been."

"When did he come back here?"

"First time was not long after Pearl Harbor. Came all the way back here to join the Army."

"Wait a minute. Let me get this right. The government stole his reservation and refused to recognize his tribe, but he signed up to defend the country that had treated him like crap?"

"He did. I don't know where he went after the war, but he showed up back here again about eight years ago. Went to work at the salt mine out there in Amboy. Worked there all week. Lived in the barracks building. On the weekends, he caught the Greyhound to Smoke Tree and then hitched out here where he started building his shack."

"Out of what?"

"Out of anything he could scrounge."

"But you said there is no road to his place."

"There isn't. He hauled everything in on foot. And I misspoke when I called it a shack. From what I hear, it's more like a lean-to. But it's shelter, and it's where Joe lives."

"Does he still work in Amboy?"

"Nope. Quit once he got his place done."

"How does he live?"

"Joe never lost touch with the old ways. He knows how to live off the land."

"Live off the land? This is not what I'd call land. This is a God-forsaken, barren desert that will barely support a lizard."

"It's not barren to someone like Joe. He makes cakes out of chia seeds, roasts agave hearts, makes meal out of mesquite beans he gets down by the river."

"That's it?"

"He hunts. He snares birds and ground squirrels – shoots jackrabbits."

"He eats jackrabbits?"

"Sure. Sometimes he turns them into jerky. Hunts burro deer, too."

"What's a burro deer?"

"A small version of a mule deer. Most people have never even seen one, but Joe can find them. And he shoots burros, too. There are lots of them out here. Left over from when there was prospecting and mining out in this country."

"People mined out here?

"Yeah, Wyatt Earp, among others. That's why that little bump in the road before Parker is named Earp."

"Good God. Sounds like this Joe has a hard life."

"I suppose he has. But I'll bet he's healthier than you or me. Lots of plants in his diet, only lean meat from the game he shoots, lots of exercise scrounging for his food. Doesn't smoke, doesn't drink."

"Does he ever come into town?"

"Yeah. Comes into Smoke Tree or goes into Parker from time to time. Works a bit now and then. Man is one heck of a carpenter. When he makes a few dollars, he buys some canned fruit. Really partial to canned peaches. Says it's his one weakness."

"How do you know so much about him, Lieutenant?"

"Oh, I've talked to Joe quite a few times over the years. He's a good guy. Just doesn't have much use for civilization."

"How do you know so much about all these Indians? The other day, I heard you telling Fred all about the Mojaves."

"It's my job to know everything about everybody out here."

"That's a lot of people."

"Not really. Look at our area. From Ludlow on the west, south to the Riverside County line, and north from Ludlow to the Nevada state line. Then along the Nevada border to the Colorado River and then down the California side of the river to Earp.

Granted, it's a lot of land. You could put a few small states, plus Los Angeles, Chicago, Atlanta, and San Francisco inside it and still have room left over. But if you added up all the people living in that area, it would be less than ten thousand, a lot less. The fewer people you have, the more important they are. Everyone out here is important. And the department has to balance their needs with the thousands and thousands of people who come through on Route 66 every day, not to mention those on 95 coming up from Arizona to Nevada and 91 from Barstow to Vegas. Every one of the people passing through is a possible problem, not only if they come into conflict with the locals but if they break down or wander off the road into the desert and get lost, especially in the summer. You know, sometimes the people we get called out to search for are dead before we can find them."

"Lieutenant, can I ask you something?"

"Go ahead."

"How long you been stationed in Smoke Tree?"

"Ever since I started. I asked for this assignment."

"What are you going to do when you make captain?"

"Turn it down. Substation commander is a lieutenant's spot. If I take captain, they'll transfer me, and I intend to stay right here my whole career. I was born and raised here. Only left for the Korean War."

"Well, I guess someone has to do it. Me, I can't wait to get back to San Bernardino."

"To each his own, Andy. But look at that beautiful sky. Look at those stars. Listen to the blessed quiet. Breathe that clean air. Man, I wouldn't live in San Bernardino under all that smog with all those crazy people for anything."

"You've got a point there, Lieutenant. Sometimes this place is all right. But in August when it's a hundred and two at midnight? And February with that damned wind and the air so dry your nose bleeds, your lips crack and the static electricity jumps a foot when you walk across a carpet? Not for this boy."

The two sat quietly for a while.

"Lieutenant, are we going to try to keep track of this guy tonight?"

"No. We just want to be sure he's not going to come in after us. By now, he's desperate for a drink. I'll watch from now to eleven. Then you take until two, and then I'll take over until dawn. You go ahead and get some sleep now."

Horse moved away in the darkness toward where they had last seen Vickers.

He sat on the crest of the hill alone with his thoughts. He thought about Esperanza, the wonderful wife he loved beyond all reason. He hoped she wasn't worried about him right now, even though he knew she would be. He wondered what he had ever done to earn the love and devotion of such a woman. Such a good heart. So kind and so strong. He remembered the first time he had ever seen her.

It was on the first day of class at Smoke Tree Junior High. The Smoke Tree Unified School district had three elementary schools – one for the entire west side of town and one for the east. As a result, even though Smoke Tree was a small community, many of the youngsters in town were not thrown together until the three elementary schools dumped into the junior high.

On his first day in seventh grade, Horse was struggling to open his first-ever school locker when he looked up to see a beautiful girl in a bright blue dress. She smiled as she skipped down the walkway toward him with two friends, her thickly braided black hair bouncing as she moved. She had a wonderful smile, and her eyes shone as she laughed at something one of them had said.

Horse could never remember who the two friends were because his eyes zeroed in on Esperanza with such intensity her friends had disappeared as far as he was concerned. In that instant, he made up his mind she would someday be his girlfriend.

By Thanksgiving, they were inseparable. They held hands together between every class and at lunch. For Horse, perhaps it was the absence of a father who had enlisted two months after Pearl Harbor and died in Europe, but whatever it was, Esperanza filled a void in Horse's heart. Filled it to overflowing.

At first, the other boys in the class teased Horse about his infatuation. They quickly discovered he didn't care. They also discovered that if they crossed an invisible line by making disparaging or off-color remarks about Esperanza, they were in for an unpleasant experience. It was like being set upon by a dust devil with fists and elbows: win, lose, or draw; it was not something they wanted to do again.

By the time they were sophomores at Smoke Tree High, it was clear to everyone that Horse and Esperanza intended to spend their lives together. Their friends all thought they would marry right after graduation. But Horse was committed to helping his mother raise his younger brother and sister, and his job as a yard clerk for the Santa Fe did not provide enough money to support two households. Esperanza had a job at the Foster's Freeze, but it did not pay enough to help much. Horse and Esperanza had to settle for being together every moment they could steal from their respective jobs and family obligations.

Then, in 1950, war broke out in Korea, and Horse was drafted.

Draftees from San Bernardino County were ordered to assemble at the Orange Show Fairgrounds in San Bernardino to be bused to Los Angeles for induction. Esperanza drove him to the Santa Fe depot in Smoke Tree and held his hand while they waited for the train to San Bernardino. When it came, she kissed him long and hard one last time. It was the loneliest train ride of his life, knowing every mile took him farther from the woman he loved.

Esperanza not only waited for him, but she also wrote him a letter every day he was gone. Horse took a lot of ribbing during his stateside training about this constant stream of mail, but when he reached his unit in Korea, everyone was aware each letter a soldier was reading might be his last.

Horse returned home in 1952 a very different man than the one who had stood on that train platform two years before. But one thing had not changed: his love for Esperanza. And even though the Santa Fe was obligated to re-hire him and give him his seniority rights for the years he had been away, he no longer wanted to work there. Things had changed.

For one thing, his younger brother and sister were out of the house and the economic need was not so great. For another, he had spent some time as an M.P. in Korea and found that he liked the work. He didn't want to be associated with the Smoke Tree Police Department, but he had heard good things about changes at the San Bernardino County Sheriff's Department under Sheriff Frank Bland. He applied to the academy and was accepted.

In 1953, he graduated from the academy and was given the duty assignment he requested: Smoke Tree Substation. Within a month of the assignment, he and Esperanza were married. The marriage was everything he had dreamed it would be while he suffered through Korea.

His only regret was that he and Esperanza had no children. Mumps when he was a teenager had removed that possibility. The fact that Esperanza knew that when she married him but married him anyway despite how much she loved children deepened his love for her. They were beginning to talk seriously about adoption. God knew the orphanages in Mexico were filled with children who needed homes.

He thought about the dead woman in the trunk of the car. The desperate, defeated, sorrowful look in her eyes. He thought about the man who killed her, hiding out there in the darkness. He couldn't wait for first light so he could hunt him down.

He ended up letting Andy have an extra hour of sleep. Horse wasn't tired, and he enjoyed the incredible canopy of the night sky, especially the occasional shooting star. When the eastern horizon began to brighten ahead of the moonrise after midnight, he returned to camp and woke Andy.

When Andy had moved off toward the edge of the hill, Horse unstrapped his gun and took off his boots. He rolled the gun and holster in its belt and put it beside the blanket he positioned so that his feet pointed downhill. He pulled the blanket over himself and was asleep in minutes.

DAY THREE

When Harvey awoke, the cold wind had picked up out of the north and was rustling the leaves on the desert willows in the wash. He realized the moon had risen above the mountains in front of him. He stood up and looked around. He hadn't meant to fall asleep, but now he was sure whoever was following him had stopped for the night. He thought again about the water they were probably carrying and realized they were just going to trail him and wait him out until he couldn't go on.

But how in the heck had they followed him? He had been very careful, making that false trail, walking down those compressed rocks, and then running down the middle of the highway. How had they picked up his tracks?

At least he'd slowed them down. It had taken them a long time to catch up with him. But if they hadn't followed him in the dark, they might come on ahead now that the moon was up. It was putting out enough light that he could see to walk. He decided to get moving and put more distance between him and them, and even more, if they were still sleeping.

He got to his feet. Christ, he felt like he was a hundred years old! He was thirstier than ever. He tried putting a pebble under his tongue, but that just made his mouth taste like dirt. Dry dirt.

The moon played cruel tricks on him as he moved onward in the broad wash. Several times, moonlight reflecting off rocks flaked with quartz or mica fooled him into thinking he had found a pool of water. Each time he realized he was wrong, he vowed not to get his hopes up again. Logically, he knew there was no water in this dry wash. But he couldn't help it. Frankie Lane's "Cool Water" began playing endlessly in his head.

★ ★ ★

Horse came awake with the uneasy feeling he was being watched. He made out a dark figure sitting off to his right. He sat up quickly, reaching for his gun.

"Easy, Horse," came a voice from the dark. "Moved your gun so you wouldn't shoot me. You deputies can be jumpy."

Horse relaxed. "Especially when we wake up in the middle of the night with someone sitting next to us. How long you been sitting there, Joe?"

"A bit. Who's the lad up the hill?"

"Andy Chesney. Was he sleeping when you came in?"

"No. Awake, sort of."

"How close did you get to him?"

"Close enough to hear him breathing and know he was awake."

"You come down from your place?"

"Nope. Hitched a ride from Smoke Tree. Guy going to the night shift at the compressor station. Walked the rest of the way in."

"How'd you find us?"

"Smelled cigarette smoke 'bout a half-mile out. Saw a match when your deputy lit up again. Scouted around. Found your horses. Found you."

"You really are good, Joe. I had no idea you were here. I'm wide awake now. Let's go send Andy down and let him sleep. I'd like to talk to you."

Horse pushed his blanket aside. He shook out his boots in case a scorpion or a centipede had crawled in. He put them on and retrieved his gun from Joe. They walked up the hill.

"Come on in, Andy. I'll take over. You go ahead and get some sleep."

Andy got up and started down the hill. He suddenly realized somebody was standing behind Horse in the moonlight. He reached for his gun.

"Horse, behind you! Lookout!

"Easy, Andy, easy. He's a friendly. Come on down."

When Andy was beside them, Horse said, "this is Joe Medrano. Joe, Andy Chesney."

Andy held out his hand.

"Pleased to meet you, sir."

Joe touched Andy's hand briefly and nodded.

"Go get some sleep. Joe and I are going to talk a while."

Andy went down the hill. Joe and Horse moved to the crest and sat down facing northeast. Neither one spoke. They watched the moon climb higher in the sky.

After a long time, Horse broke the silence.

"Joe, we're after a guy We think he killed his wife. We know for sure he shot an inspector at the station in Vidal."

"Why do you think he killed his wife?

"Her body was in the trunk of his car."

"Clue."

"That's right."

"When'd you see him last?"

"Just before dark." Horse pointed to the northeast. "He was in the wash out there. We know he has a gun. Little .22 pistol. Popped a round off our direction about three this afternoon. What he doesn't have is food or water."

"Gonna wait him out?"

"Yeah. Don't want to shoot him if we don't have to."

"What's his name?"

"Harvey Vickers."

"Mean, sneaky guy, squinty eyes1`?"

"That's more than I know about him."

"Works at Bondurant's Market in Parker. Wife is Rose Lynne."

"Blonde hair, blue eyes? A little chubby?"

"Yep. Shoot her?"

"Huh-uh. Strangled her. And he beat her up real bad first.

He was going to drive somewhere. I don't know why. When he stopped at the inspection station, an inspector told him to get out of his car and open the trunk. He shot the inspector instead and drove off."

"Inspector dead?"

"No."

"Why's Vickers on foot?"

"Car quit for some reason."

They sat again without speaking.

"Headed more or less my way?"

"I'm not quite sure where your place is. I doubt he does either, but he might find it."

"Might."

They sat for a while longer.

"Need to know what you've got in the way of guns out there, Joe."

"Single-shot .22 for rabbits. A .30-06."

"Scope or iron sights?"

"Iron."

"That's it? No shotgun?"

"Shells cost too much. What's the plan?"

"Keep following him in the morning. If we think he's going to wind up at your place, maybe we can get there ahead of him."

"Trouble if he gets my deer gun."

"Could be. Hope he hasn't moved on in the night."

"Has. Circled before I came in. Big circle. Not there."

"Well, I don't want to stumble on the guy in the night. The young deputy and I will set out in the morning."

"I can watch. You sleep."

"Nah. I'm done for the night. Let's just wait a while. We'll wake Andy after a bit. Be ready to start at first light. Joe, you like scrambled eggs?"

"Sure."

"Got some C-rations. We'll have eggs and coffee before we get moving."

In a few minutes, the immense silence of the desert settled around them. The wind began to pick up from the north. The two men sat unmoving on the hill, each thinking his own thoughts. Looking out at moonlit country so unchanged by time, it would not have seemed surprising to see some neolithic hunter-gatherer moving carefully over the land, intent on a task essential to survival.

★ ★ ★

Harvey continued to move in the moonlight. Transitioning from get-away mode to survival mode, he was not moving very fast. As the terrain steepened, the wash was narrower and more choked with catclaw. He thought there might be a chance of finding water, so he climbed higher.

An hour later, the wash became a deep canyon full of obstacles. He found himself clambering over piles of rocks and running into larger and larger boulders. He sat down to rest for a moment against one of the boulders. Within minutes, he was asleep again.

He woke with a start, and the moon was much higher in the sky. He hadn't meant to fall asleep. He had to keep moving! With some difficulty, he got to his feet and moved on.

He had not walked long before the sky grew lighter in the east. He scrambled to the top of a pile of small boulders and looked at the ground rising in front of him. He saw the canyon was getting deeper and rising more vertically. He also realized it would eventually terminate against a cliff's face. He decided to climb out over the steep hill on the south side of the canyon.

Sunrise found him traversing the face of the hill. It was becoming more and more of a struggle to force himself onward. He had just about decided to sit down and wait for his pursuers to take him into custody when something farther up the hill to the southeast caught his eye. Something not natural. Something brightly colored. Puzzled, he moved toward it.

After another fifty yards, he realized he was looking at a door! A door painted turquoise. Above the door was a roof of some sort. Suddenly, his feet didn't bother him so much. Maybe there was water there. Even if someone was behind the door, they probably weren't awake yet. And he had a gun!

They were about to have company.

★ ★ ★

Just before sunrise, Horse and Joe went down the hill and awakened Andy. Horse made a small fire ring and built a fire. He filled a mess cup with water and set it on the rocks to boil while he opened two cans of scrambled eggs from the C-rations.

"Andy, go back down the hill and fetch us up a ham slices meal. In my saddlebags, you'll find a couple of loops of picture wire. Bring those up too."

Horse pushed the opened cans of chopped eggs to the edge of the fire. When Andy came back, Horse opened the ham slices and pushed them next to the eggs. He put the wire Andy handed him on the ground. He walked to a creosote bush where he cut three, four-inch pieces of wood and put them in his pocket.

After they were done sharing the food, he stirred the instant coffee and all the sugar from all five meals into the water.

"That's a lot of sugar, Lieutenant."

"Believe me, Andy, you don't want to try to drink U.S. Army instant coffee without lots of sugar."

While he waited for the water to boil, he took the empty food cans and made coffee cups from them by wrapping picture wire around the tops and bottoms of the cans, then twisting the ends of the wires around the pieces of wood.

Andy sat looking at Joe. From what Horse had told him about the man's service in World War II, he should be in his late thirties or early to mid-forties, but it was hard to be sure. His long hair was thick and black. His face was completely unlined. His dark eyes gave away nothing. Only his hands told a different story. They were the hands of a man who had seen lots of hard labor.

Joe looked at Andy. Andy looked away, embarrassed at being caught staring.

"From the South?" Joe asked.

"Sort of. My family moved to Fontana when I was a kid. Guess I still have some of that accent."

"Whereabouts?"

"Alabama. My daddy worked the mills in Birmingham. Thought the opportunities might be better with Kaiser. Better opportunities for us kids too, in California."

"Served with some southern boys Got something you might like."

Joe walked off over the hillside until he found the small plant he was looking for. He uprooted it and brought it back. Sitting beside the fire, he cleaned the dirt off the roots, peeled some slivers off them with his knife and dropped them into the boiling coffee.

When Andy took his first sip, his face creased with a smile.

"I'll be damned. Chicory"

They drank the flavored, sweetened coffee from the cobbled-together mugs and ate the chocolate squares from the three meals.

"Mr. Medrano, can I ask you something?"

"Can ask."

"How'd you come in last night without me hearing you?"

"Trick I learned."

"How close were you to me?"

"Coulda touched you."

"I'm embarrassed. I thought I was pretty alert."

"Mimbres Apache, a Ute from Colorado and me went inside Japanese perimeters. Made sure lots of Tojo's boys never woke up."

Joe was a man of small stature, maybe five foot seven and one hundred and thirty-five pounds, but the forearms extending from his rolled-up, flannel shirt sleeves were knotted with muscle. Andy could imagine him slipping silently past enemy sentries in the Pacific in the night. He shuddered to think such a deadly man had been so close to him without him knowing it.

Horse started gathering the cans and the boxes.

"Notice you did that last night, Lieutenant. Why not just leave it? Probably won't be anybody on this hillside for another fifty years."

"I don't leave junk on the desert. It might be dusty, but it's clean, and everything lasts forever. You can still find K-ration cans and commo wire from Patton's army when they trained over in Ward Valley in 1940."

They helped Horse pick up the trash and carry it down the hill. Horse flattened the cans and boxes and put everything in his saddlebags.

"Joe, we're going to set off after Vickers."

"Like to help. Wife, nice lady."

"I'm not supposed to involve civilians."

"Don't have to. Walk in front of you. Happen onto his track, follow it. Curious, who's in my neighborhood."

"Okay. But if you see him, come back to us."

"Okay."

"Lieutenant, are we going to take the horses?"

"Better not. It's going to get real rough up ahead. Horses would be more trouble than help. We'll pick them up on our way back."

They watered the horses and moved them so they could graze on what sparse desert grasses and shrubs they could find. When they finished, Joe was gone. They hadn't heard him leave. They picked up their canteens and rifles and set out. At the top of the rise, they could see Joe far out in front of them. He was heading northeast, well beyond where they had last seen Vickers the night before. They set off after him.

Trampas Wash was rough country. Not only was the wash beginning to incline sharply to the east, but it was also filled with long, rocky stretches that had apparently allowed Vickers to stay out of the sand where he might have left tracks.

The land told a story of violent events. Rare but powerful floodwaters had poured swiftly off the distant, steep escarpment. Flash floods had scoured the land, uprooting trees, tumbling rocks, and even boulders down the washes.

Given the conditions, Horse was amazed by how easily Joe followed the trail. Even though Vickers had apparently moved in a zig-zag fashion to take advantage of rocky stretches, Joe moved steadily. Occasionally, he would kneel down for a few moments, and now and then, he would drop onto his stomach to look at something with his eyes at ground level. But by and large, he moved quickly and with confidence. Horse saw none of the casting arcs he had found it necessary to make because he kept losing the trail.

As the wash approached the eastern escarpment of the Chemehuevi Mountains, it became a deep canyon. There was red, volcanic material mixed in with the granite. Thousands and thousands of flash floods had deposited a jumble of rocks of all sizes and compositions, from large boulders to pea gravel. The going was more difficult because the canyon was also jammed with catclaw acacia, known locally as 'wait-a-minute bush.'

As they climbed onward, desert lavender and Arizona lupine appeared, along with desert agave, more and more barrel cactus, and teddy bear cholla. Bigelow nolinas, an elegant cousin of the bayonet yucca with thinner spikes, were scattered throughout the pockets of sand between the rocks.

Well out in front of them, Joe suddenly took an angle off to the south and began to climb quickly up the north-facing side of the canyon. Even though the canyon was steep, Joe seemed to flow effortlessly over the rugged terrain. When he was near the top, he dropped onto his stomach, low-crawled over the edge, and disappeared.

Fifteen minutes later, Horse and Andy had just reached the point where Joe had left the bottom of the canyon when they heard someone whistle softly behind them. Andy whirled around so quickly that he almost lost his balance.

"Jesus, Mr. Medrano. You scared the pants off me."

"Deputy, shared food, coffee. I'm Joe."

"What did you see up there?" asked Horse.

"Not good. Headed my place. Get those guns."

"No way we can get ahead of him? Get there first?"

"No. Too long, climb above him. Be there before we can cut him off."

"Then let's stay together and keep following him. You stay behind Andy and me. We've got rifles."

"Okay."

The three men began to climb out of the canyon When they neared the ridge, Joe touched Horse's shoulder.

"Best not silhouette ourselves."

All three men crawled over the edge and down the other side.

★ ★ ★

As Harvey got closer to the door, he was convinced nobody was home. No smoke on display. No sounds in the still morning air. His spirits fell as he crept cautiously forward with his gun in his hand. Maybe the place was abandoned. It sure didn't look like much.

The door was hinged to some kind of a post and lintel, but the walls were of brush lashed together and plastered with mud. The roof had been made with the same woven brush, but no mud was plastered on top of it.

There was a handle on the door. Higher up, the door was held closed by a hook. That meant there was no one inside unless parents had locked a child in until they got back from somewhere. He could handle a kid. He unhooked the door, slowly pulled it open, and stepped inside. There was not much light in the room.

As his eyes adjusted, he realized there was a large fire ring just inside the door. The open weave of the brush on the roof would allow the smoke to get out. Massive eyebolts, the kind used to hook cables and turnbuckles that supported telephone poles, had been cemented into the ground. A large metal rod was sticking through the holes. It could be used to hang pots over the fire or serve as a spit for roasting meat. Walking behind the large fire pit, he saw a single, large room had been excavated from the hillside.

In the middle of the space was a large, hand-made table. There was a chair at the table. The only things on the table were a water jug and a clay bowl with a lid. Harvey shoved his gun into his belt and picked up the jug. He uncapped it and began to gulp the water as fast as he could swallow without choking. He was careful not to spill any. He wanted it all!

Within moments, the jug was three-quarters empty. He put it on the table and took the lid off the clay bowl. It was filled with things that looked like small, thick pancakes. He began stuffing them in his mouth. There was no salt or sugar in them, nor any other seasoning, but they were the best food he had ever eaten. The cakes were dry, and he was eating so fast he nearly choked. He picked up the water jug to wash them down.

When the cakes and the water were gone, he felt much better. To think that he had been just about ready to call it quits a short time ago! Thank God for turquoise doors.

Beside the large table was a smaller one. There were pots, skillets, and a large, blue-enamel coffee pot on the table. There was also a single plate and a mug. Next to the smaller table was a large cabinet. Harvey walked over and opened the doors. The cabinet was filled with carpentry and wood-carving tools.

Harvey walked deeper into the room. The floor was dirt but cleanly swept. Well back into the hillside, against the back wall, was a single army cot with wool blankets. There was no pillow. Vickers walked closer. On the floor to the right side of the cot was a bushel basket and a large wooden box. The bushel basket had items of neatly folded clothing. The wooden box was full of books. On the floor next to the box were two oil lamps. Next to the lamps was a large metal container that probably contained kerosene.

Beside the oil lamps, two rifles leaned against the wall. One was a cheap J.C. Penny, single-shot .22. The other was a .30-06. He picked up the .30-06. It was the 1903 Springfield model. When he pulled back the bolt, the action was smooth and well-oiled. The magazine was empty.

He carried the rifle over to the cabinet and searched for ammunition. He found a wooden box with a sliding lid. There were hundreds of .22 cartridges, but only a handful for the .30-06. He put them all in his pocket.

Now that he had a full belly, what Harvey really wanted to do was to lie down on the cot and sleep. But he knew the people coming for him were probably not far behind. He moved back to the big table and sat down. He snapped five cartridges into the rifle's magazine, pushed the bolt forward, and locked it into place. That left four cartridges in his pocket. He moved the safety to the 'on' position and went outside.

★ ★ ★

"Turquoise up there? My door. Open partway. Left it closed. Guy has my guns."

Horse focused his binoculars on the door.

"Lord, Joe, you've got good eyes. I could barely see the door, much less tell whether it was open or not. I can't see him up there, but then I can't see all the ground leading up to your place because of the curve of the hill. But he's going to have the same problem. If he's up there somewhere, I can't see him, but he can't see us either."

"Little dip twenty yards in front of my place."

"So, what do we do now?" asked Andy.

"Joe, I assume there's food and water at your place."

"Water and chia cakes."

"There goes waiting him out. So, first thing we need to do is find out if he's up there or if he's left and is heading toward Lake Havasu."

Horse put his binoculars on the ground and took off his jacket.

"Andy, help me gather up a bunch of small bushes. I want the whole bushes. Use your knife to cut them off at the ground. We're going to make a dummy."

They gathered a pile. Horse lay his rifle on his jacket with the butt of the stock above the neck. He stacked bushes around the rifle. When he was finished, he zipped his jacket over everything. Then he picked up the jacket and rifle and put his hat over the protruding butt.

"Pretty good scarecrow."

"You're gonna stick that up and see if he shoots at it, Lieutenant?"

"Yeah."

"What if he hits your rifle?"

"Better than hitting one of us. Besides, it's over two hundred yards up to where he might be, and he's got iron sights. But more importantly, he's shooting downhill on a sharp angle, and I'm betting he'll shoot high."

"I hope you're right."

"We'll know in a minute."

Horse took his creation a little farther up the hill. Then he lay down on his side and inched his way higher. Just before he would have been exposed to view from above, he stopped and rolled onto his back. Holding his rifle by the barrel, he hoisted it into the air.

A few seconds later, there was a loud 'craaack' overhead, followed shortly by the echo of a rifle shot rolling like thunder down the canyon. Horse instantly pushed up hard on the rifle barrel. His hat went flying off the stock as he pulled the rifle down. The canyon wrens that had been singing all morning went silent.

Sweat popped out on Horse's forehead. Even though he thought he had been prepared for it, the sound had yanked him back to the snow-covered, round hills and broad valleys of Korea. His head filled with unwanted images, and just for a moment, he thought he could hear the echo of bugles. He shook his head to chase away the demons, but he knew they would be in his dreams before the week was out.

"I'd say he was up there. That bullet passed overhead. I don't know how far, but it sure didn't hit the ground in front of us."

"I've never heard a bullet go over my head before. That's a nasty sound."

"I take it you've never done military service."

"No sir."

"Well, you're about to learn an infantry tactic. It's called 'fire and movement.

Joe, I'm sure you did lots of that in the Pacific. Right?"

But Joe wasn't there.

★ ★ ★

There was a low spot in front of the house. Harvey walked back down the way he had come until the hill began to slope sharply away from him. He got down on the ground and crawled forward, pushing the rifle in front of himself until he could see a good distance down the hill. He pulled the rifle to his shoulder and rested it on the ground. Looking through the peep sight, he lined up the front blade with the spot where he thought whoever was pursuing him would appear.

He clicked the safety to the 'off' position and settled down to wait. With his stomach full of food and water, he was afraid he would nod off if someone didn't show up soon.

He didn't have to wait long.

A white hat and the upper torso of a man came into view. The figure seemed to be moving from side to side as though trying to find a clear line of sight. Harvey held a little high to compensate for the distance, took the slack out of the trigger, and squeezed off a round. The rifle slammed against his shoulder. Dust flew up off the ground. He was surprised by the thunderous sound of the shot as it echoed down the canyon.

The white hat flew up in the air. The man disappeared.

Hot damn! He'd hit him. What a shot!

Heart pounding with exhilaration, he worked the bolt, shoved another round into the chamber, and waited to see if anyone else showed up.

★ ★ ★

"Andy, how many rounds have you got for that rifle?"

The deputy took off his hat, reached in his pocket, and dumped the rounds into the hat.

"Five in the magazine and twelve more here."

"Okay, that's enough to do what we're going to do and have some left over if you need them. So, Andy, 'fire and movement.' Just like in those western movies you like where they yell, "Cover me!" and take off running.

Here's how we're going to do it.

First move, you're going to stay below Vickers' line of sight and slide off to your right about fifty yards. When you've gone that far, crawl carefully up the hill to where you can just see that blue door, but no higher. If all you can see is the door, he won't be able to see you from where he is.

Push your rifle forward and get ready to shoot over his head. When you're ready, wave at me. When I wave back, put a round over his head. Work the bolt, count to three, and shoot again.

Here's what I'm relying on. This guy has probably never heard a supersonic round go over his head. I flat guarantee you his butt will pucker up, and he'll eat dirt. By the time he thinks about looking up, the second round will go over, and he'll stay down a while.

When you shoot that first round, I'll take off running for that pile of rocks above us and to our left. When I get there, I'll wait for a few minutes. It'll take that long before he has any interest in sticking his head above the ground.

I'll wave to you. When I do, get ready to run. When I shoot, you take off for a spot about twenty-five yards to the right and a little farther up the hill. Whether you're there or not, when you hear my second shot, stop and get down. If you can't see that blue door, wait a few minutes and then crawl up the hill until you can see it again. As soon as you can see any part of the door, stop. I don't want you where he can get you in his sights.

Wave at me when you're ready to shoot, then follow the same sequence you did the first time you shot. When you shoot, I'll run farther up the hill.

When I get to my second spot, because of the sloping curve of the hill, we won't be able to see each other anymore. I'll wait a few minutes for you to get ready, and then I'll shoot again. Same pattern. You take off on the first shot, moving farther to your right but no farther up the hill this time. The hill's angle will change during your run, and I want to be sure you stay in an enfilade position."

"What's enfilade?"

"Enfilade means Andy doesn't get shot. When you reach that next position, reload. Then you're going to do something a little different the third time you shoot. By then, he may be figuring out the pattern and be ready to pop up after your second shot. And the way I see the terrain and the cover up there, my third move may take a little longer. I don't want to get caught in the open, so work the bolt as fast as you can after your second shot and shoot two more times. Then reload again.

By the time I get to that next spot, we should have Vickers almost triangulated. I may even be able to see him. I'll shoot two more times, and you move again. After that, we should have him pinned. He won't be able to go forward, and he won't be able to go back.

Once you're in position and I've had time to see how things look from there, I'll decide what to do next. No matter what I do, unless I tell you to come on up the hill, you stay put. Got all that?"

"Yes, sir."

Horse crawled forward and brought his rifle to his shoulder He looked through the scope toward where he thought Vickers was. Even though he didn't think Vickers could see Andy below the line of the hill, Horse was afraid if the man suddenly stood up, he might be able to see Andy moving. If Vickers stood up and started to bring up his rifle, Horse was going to kill him.

"Okay, Andy. Start moving."

Andy moved off to the right. When he was about where he thought Horse wanted him to stop, he crawled forward, pushing his rifle in front of him until he could see the blue door. He waved at Horse. When Horse waved back, Andy aimed above where he thought Vickers was and squeezed off a round.

As the sound of Andy's shot boomed through the canyon, Horse sprinted for the rock pile with his rifle in one hand. He was almost there when he heard the second round. He made it to cover without any shots fired his way.

He waited for a few moments and then fired his first round. He worked the bolt, counted to three, and fired a second time.

He peered around the rocks. Andy was in his new position. Horse got ready to run again. Andy fired. Horse moved again. He made the second position safely.

Once again, Horse fired twice while Andy moved.

When Andy got to his new position, there was a pause while he reloaded. Because of the angle of the hill, Horse could no longer see him. Horse looked up the hill. The next place he had to reach to find cover looked a long way away. He wished he had told Andy to shoot all five rounds instead of just four. Oh well. Couldn't change the plan now.

★ ★ ★

Harvey kept looking over the barrel of his rifle. He didn't see anyone moving. Maybe there had only been one guy, and he had put him down. Head shot! He had a pretty good idea what a .30-06 would do to a human head. Teach him to mess with Harvey Vickers!

Suddenly, it sounded like God had ripped a piece out of the sky above his head. He flattened himself against the ground just as the rolling thunder of a rifle shot reached him.

What the hell!? What the hell!

He was thinking about lifting his head when the terrible tearing sound came again. He hugged the ground as if having a love affair with the dirt as the sound rolled through the canyon.

It was a few minutes before he could muster the courage to lift his head and look down the hill over his rifle barrel. There was nothing moving. As he scanned the terrain, the terrible sound of the sky being shredded came again. He embraced the ground, trembling. Another shot passed above him.

"Stop it, you bastards," he tried to scream.

But his throat was so constricted by fear, only a croak came out. He kept his head down longer. He was thinking about trying to run to a safer spot when the bullets came again. 'Craaack! Boom!' Pause. 'Craaack! Boom!' Pause.

Even though he was nearly paralyzed with fear, a thought pierced his panic. There was a pattern! One shot, then a long pause, then a second shot. Then silence for a few minutes, then the pattern was repeated.

Trembling against the ground, he waited, determined to pay close attention to the next sequence.

That terrible 'craaack,' followed by the boom. Pause. Then 'craaack,' 'boom' again.

What was that about? Oh, hell. There were two of them. One was shooting while the other one moved. They were closing in on him. So there had been three! He'd killed one, and now the other two were going to gun him down. It wasn't fair! Two against one. Why couldn't he ever catch a break?

But he came up with a plan! When the next sequence came, he would be ready. After the second shot, he would pop up and catch one of them running and put him down. That would change the odds!

The supersonic ripping sound tore the sky apart again. He waited.

At the second "craaack,' he forced himself to lift his head and look over his sights. Just as he did, a third round screamed overhead. He scrunched into the dirt, screaming in frustration. As he did, a fourth round passed over.

★ ★ ★

When Andy fired the first shot in his third sequence, Horse was waiting with his rifle slung crosswise over his back. As the round headed up the hill, Horse sprinted. He dug hard, arms pumping, hands free in case he fell and had to catch himself.

Shortly after Andy's second shot, Horse caught movement up the hill as he ran. Vickers had figured it out, but he seemed to be looking straight down the hill. He didn't realize Horse was flanking him, but he might at any moment. Horse almost dropped to his hands and knees, but then Andy's third shot boomed out. Vickers disappeared like a prairie dog ducking into its hole.

By the time the fourth shot echoed, Horse had reached the cover where he thought he might have the angle he needed. He paused a few minutes to slow his breathing. He reloaded his magazine, slowly eased his rifle forward, and peered through the scope.

He could see the heel of the man's right foot. He settled the crosshairs on the ground a few feet to the left of the shoe and got ready to shoot. Just as he was taking the slack out of the trigger, he caught movement in the upper right and corner of his scope. He eased the pressure off the trigger and moved the rifle.

It was Chemehuevi Joe! He had worked his way up the far right downslope side of the canyon to a point above Vickers, and he was moving carefully down the hill toward the man. Good Lord! If Vickers heard him and turned around, Joe was a dead man!

Horse fired four rounds high and to the left of Vickers as fast as he could work the bolt. As the explosions died to a distant echo, he put the scope where he had last seen Chemehuevi Joe. Joe was gone. He focused on where he had seen Vickers' foot. It was no longer visible.

★ ★ ★

In the instant before the third shot came and forced his head down, Harvey had picked up movement out of the corner of his eye. It was in front of him and to his right. His plan would've worked if it hadn't been for those third and fourth shots. He lay in the deafening silence of the desert morning, unsure what he should do next.

The guy above him probably didn't know he had been seen. He also might be resting from his run up the hill. Tentatively, Harvey pushed his rifle barrel to the right and got ready to lift his head so he could shoot that direction.

Then four rounds slammed into the ground to his right. Maybe the guy didn't know exactly where he was, and maybe those four rounds had emptied his gun!

He was lifting his head to look when something slammed into his back. A hand seized the collar of his shirt and yanked his head backward. At the same time, he felt the point of something very sharp against his throat.

"Don't move. Skinning knife. Kill you quick. Push the rifle down the hill."

Struggling to control his panic, Harvey did as he was told.

"Spread your arms, palms down.

Heart hammering, he spread his arms. He tried to speak. It came out as a squeak.

"Who are you."

The man ignored his question.

"Left-handed, get the gun stuck in your belt. Drop it beside you."

When Harvey had done that, the voice came again.

"Pick it up by the barrel. Throw it away from you."

The entire time Harvey was complying, the pressure applied to the knife against his throat stayed exactly the same. Whoever was behind him was very calm.

"Arms straight in front of you, palms down."

When he had stretched his arms out straight, the man behind him suddenly stood up, pulling Harvey to his knees.

"Hands in your pockets. Make fists."

"What?"

"Fists. In your pockets. Now, stand up. Don't be stupid."

"Oaky, okay. I won't."

"Shut up."

Harvey got slowly to his feet. It was not easy with his fists jammed into his pockets and his legs wobbling, but he was careful not to fall. He was convinced whoever was behind him would cut his throat if he lost his balance.

"Walk!"

The man guided Harvey in shuffling steps toward the edge of the hill.

★ ★ ★

Through his scope, Horse saw a rifle slide a few feet down the hill. Then Vickers rose to his knees. His face loomed large in the powerful scope. His eyes were jerking side to side. Horse could see a brown hand pressing the point of a long, thin-bladed knife against Vickers' throat. He couldn't see the rest of Chemehuevi Joe.

Then Vickers got very awkwardly to his feet. Horse couldn't understand why the man was having such a hard time, but when he was all the way up, Horse realized Vickers' hands were jammed deep into his pockets and balled into fists.

Vickers said something. After a pause, he said something else. Then he was turned to the side, and Horse could see Joe Medrano behind him. Joe had Vickers' collar knotted in one hand. The other hand was holding the knife. The two men began to move in small steps toward the edge of the gully Joe must have climbed out of. It looked almost like Joe was trying to teach Vickers a dance step,

Horse stood up and yelled.

"Joe! Hey, Joe! Stay there until Andy and I get there. We'll take it from here."

But Joe and Vickers kept moving in their awkward shuffle.

"Andy, come on up. Joe's got Vickers."

★ ★ ★

Harvey never thought he'd be happy to hear that voice again. It was the guy who had yelled at him yesterday. Harvey wanted someone, *anyone,* to get him away from the crazy man holding the blade to his throat. He stopped, hoping the man who had yelled was coming.

"Move!"

That voice again! It turned his knees to jelly. So flat. So cold. He struggled to get moving again. The man kept his grip on Harvey's collar. The knife stayed against his neck.

Harvey spoke again. He hated how weak his voice sounded.

"Where we going?"

"Shut up!"

The man moved the knife against Harvey's throat. He felt a trickle of blood on his skin. He almost fainted, but he managed to keep moving. The man kept shoving him forward until they reached the edge of a deep gully.

"Stop! What's down there?"

"Down where?"

"Side of the hill."

"I dunno. Dirt. Rocks. Cholla."

"Hear you like to beat up women."

"What do you mean?"

"Beat up your wife. Hurt her bad. Killed her."

"What's that got to do with you?" Harvey asked in a pleading voice.

"Nice lady. Kind. Polite."

"You knew Rose Lynne?"

There was no response. The knife stayed pressed to his neck. Harvey wished the guy who had yelled at him would get here.

The voice he was afraid of came again.

"Cholla down there."

Suddenly, Harvey realized what the man behind him had in mind.

"Hey! Hey! Wait a minute."

In one swift movement, Joe let go of Harvey's collar, pulled the knife away from his throat, and pushed him off the hill.

With his hands jammed into his pockets, there was no way Harvey could stay on his feet. Nor could he use his hands to break his fall. The best he could manage was to twist his body, so he landed on his shoulder. As soon as he did, he started to tumble, screaming, down the hill. He bounced off rocks and rolled through the cholla thicket.

★ ★ ★

Horse was over a hundred yards from Joe Medrano and Vickers when he started toward them. He thought maybe Joe hadn't heard him holler because he kept pushing Vickers forward.

As he walked toward the two men, they continued away from him with their shuffling gait. Then Horse saw Andy coming up over the side of the hill.

"Joe's got Vickers. He's headed up the hill with him. Let's catch up."

Joe Medrano and Harvey Vickers stopped. It looked to Horse like they were just standing there. Joe still had Vickers by the collar with his left hand. His right arm was still wrapped around the man's neck.

Suddenly, Joe simultaneously let go of Vickers' collar and pulled his hand away from Vickers' neck. The sun glinted off the long, slender blade of the knife as Joe pushed Vickers hard with his left hand.

Vickers disappeared over the edge of the hill. Horse heard him scream. By the time Horse and Andy reached Joe, he had put the knife away and was looking down the side of the steep gully

"What happened, Joe?"

"Guy slipped. Bounced off some rocks. Rolled through that cholla down there."

"Ouch!"

"Yeah."

"Joe, before I go down there to get him, I want you to know we're going to have to take your rifle with us, so just leave it where it is. Vickers shot at us with it. We're going to have to get prints off the gun and the brass he ejected."

"Deer season. Need my gun."

"I'll tell you what. You keep mine until I bring yours back. How's that?"

Horse carefully worked the bolt, extracted the unfired round, and handed his .30-40 Krag to Joe.

Joe hoisted the rifle and looked through the scope.

"Thanks. Always wanted a scope."

Horse took the rest of the rounds out of his pocket and handed them to Joe.

"Well, it's yours for a while."

"Little pistol over there. Probably need that too, huh?"

"Yeah. After Arizona gets done with him on the murder charge, California will probably charge him for shooting the inspector and for shooting at us, too. If they do, we'll need the pistol and the prints."

"Favor ?"

"Sure, Joe. You've earned a bushel of them."

"Court stuff. Never works for Indians. Leave me out of this."

Horse was silent for a few moments while he thought through Joe's request.

"You got it. I'd probably be in trouble with the department anyway if they knew what I'd allowed a civilian to do."

He pulled a plastic bag out of his jacket pocket and turned to his deputy.

"Andy, push a stick down the barrel of that Colt Woodsman back over there and put it in this bag without getting your prints on it. The same with the brass from the 30-06. Then pick Joe's rifle up by the sling and bring it too. I'm going down to get our prisoner. I'll meet you down where we were when Vickers shot at us."

"Okay, Horse. What about Joe?"

"What Joe?"

"The Joe standing beside you."

"Andy, here's what happened. Before you came up the hill, the prisoner surrendered. I disarmed him. But before I could get the cuffs on him, he managed to break away from me and make a run for it. Got as far as the edge of this gully. Lost his balance and rolled down through those rocks and cactus. Joe wasn't here. Vickers broke into his place up there, stole his gun, and used it to try and kill us. End of story. Do you copy?"

"Got it, Lieutenant."

"Good. Now, go get those weapons. I'll meet you down below."

Horse side-stepped down the steep gully. Vickers was at the bottom. There were cuts on his face, his shirt and pants were torn, and there were teddy bear cholla segments stuck to his arms, legs, and hands: so many of them he looked like a pin cushion. Luckily for him, there were none stuck to his face.

The only other place he didn't seem to have any was the seat of his pants. At least that's what Horse assumed because Vickers was sitting on a rock staring at the cholla segments stuck to his arms and hands.

"Are you Harvey Vickers?"

"Yeah."

"I'm Lieutenant Caballo of the San Bernardino County Sheriff's Department. Harvey Vickers, I'm arresting you for attempted murder of an agricultural inspector, attempted murder of law enforcement officers, breaking and entering, and burglary. And I'll be handing you over to the Arizona authorities. No doubt they will charge you in the murder of your wife."

"Can't you see I'm all busted up and stuck full of cholla?"

"I see you have a number of cuts. You also seem to have picked up a lot of cactus."

"What are you going to do about the cholla sticking in me?"

"Not a thing. Removing cholla is a very delicate operation. If those quills aren't pulled out on exactly the angle they went in on, they'll tear your skin to pieces. And by the way, I hope you've had a tetanus shot. You're going to need it. Classic deep-puncture wounds there."

"Get them off of me!" Vickers screamed."

"Nope. Don't know how and don't want to. I will never forget the look on your wife's face as she lay dead in the trunk of your car. I wish I could, but I think I'll see her in my dreams. No, I think you deserve every one of those spines. In fact, I'd like to take you up the hill and push you down again."

"Let me explain about my wife."

"No. I'm a California law enforcement officer. Any explanations you have about your wife, you can save for Arizona. I don't want to hear anything about what happened on the other side of the river."

"Can I ask a question?"

"If it's not about something that happened in Arizona."

"Who the hell was that guy up there?"

"What guy are you talking about?"

"Come on. The guy who held the knife to my throat. The guy you called 'Joe'. "

"I didn't see anyone."

"You must have! He made me walk to the top of the hill up there and pushed me off."

"No, that's not what happened, Vickers. I disarmed you and tried to arrest you, but you broke free and ran toward the edge of the hill where you lost your balance and went over the edge."

"Come on, man, that's crap, and you know it."

"Let me educate you. You're going to trial in Arizona for murder. They've got you nailed on the charge. The only question is what the punishment will be. So you're going to do a lot of jail time. Jail time before the trial and jail time once you're convicted. You with me so far?"

"But.."

"Just listen. Once you're inside the system, you have nothing but your story to convince the other cons you're a tough guy who shouldn't be messed with. Do you want your story to be that you were arrested after a shootout with law enforcement, a story that makes you sound like a crazy and fearless man, or do you want it to be that someone snuck up behind you when you had two loaded weapons, took both of them away from you, and pushed you in a cholla patch? What kind of a weak punk will that make you look like? If those convicts at the state penitentiary in Florence sense weakness, they'll make your life a living hell."

Vickers started to speak, then seemed to reconsider.

"Okay. On your feet. Got a long walk ahead of you."

★ ★ ★

Vickers didn't move very fast. After he and Horse met up with Andy, it took them two hours to get back to the horses. When they got there, Vickers demanded to be put on a horse. That didn't happen. It took another two hours to reach Highway 95 with the prisoner walking and Horse and Andy riding.

They put Vickers in the back seat when they got to Horse's cruiser. Vickers had to balance carefully on the edge of the seat. Any other position would have driven the cholla spines deeper into his body.

Horse helped Andy load the horses into the double trailer.

"Andy, when you get back to town, turn Canyon out into the corral. Give him some grain and make sure he has water. I'll curry him when I get home. Tell Esperanza I've gone to Parker to turn our prisoner over to Yuma County. Tell her I'll be home as soon as I can, but the paperwork and statements are going to take a while. Then go by the station and leave the rifle and the pistol in the evidence room. And Andy?"

"Yessir."

"Real good work. It was good to have you along. Couldn't have done this on my own. You're turning into a good deputy."

"Thank you, Lieutenant. I'm glad I was along. Learned some stuff."

"Good. And the part with Joe? That will be between you, me, and Joe Medrano."

"Lieutenant, do you think what Joe did was wrong?"

"No, I don't. Sometimes there's more justice outside a courtroom than in one. I think Joe gave Vickers a little taste of it. And I'll tell you something else while we're talking about the man who wasn't there. Joe probably saved the guy's life."

"How's that?"

"If it hadn't been for Joe, there's a good chance we would have shot and killed Vickers outright or wounded him so badly he'd have bled to death before we could've got him out of that canyon."

"Yeah, I see that."

"See you back in town, Deputy Chesney."

DAY FOUR

Horse didn't get back to Smoke Tree until after midnight. Esperanza was awake when he came in the door. His dinner was in the refrigerator. She warmed it while he took care of Canyon and put him away. She sat with him as he ate his dinner. He told her everything that had happened, including the part about Joe Medrano and how Horse would not be mentioning Joe in the report. After the stress of the last few days, it felt both surreal and wonderful to be in this warm house with the woman he loved.

When Horse was done, Esperanza hugged him and kissed his face.

"I'm so glad you weren't hurt. I hate it when you go off on one of these searches in the desert. And this time, someone shot at you. I'm glad Joe pushed that man down that gully."

"Me too.

That reminds me, when we get the prints off Joe's gun, I'm going to send it to Pachmayr and have them re-blue it and put a new stock on it. And I'm going to have them mount a good scope for him. It'll be expensive, but it's the least I can do. Joe saved me from having to kill someone, and that's something I never want to do again."

After his meal and a shower, he climbed into bed. He reached over and turned out the light. He thought about Joe Medrano, alone on his hillside, so close to the reservation he had once called home but could never see again.

Then Esperanza scooted up against him, and as he drifted off, he thought again about how lucky he was to have the love of this good woman.

Books in the Smoke Tree Series in the order in which
they were written following the publication
of The House of Three Murders:

Horse Hunts

Mojave Desert Sanctuary

Death on a Desert Hillside

Deep Desert Deception

The Carnival, the Cross, and the Burning Desert

Walks Always Beside You

A Desert Drowning

Woman of the Desert Moon

Smoke Tree Burning